kinanâskomitin, dad, for your gentle heart
and the medicine of your humor.

Growing up with you taught me about
our connections to the land that inspires
so much of the work that I do.

In loving memory, Clarence Flett,
Swampy Cree, Red River Métis (1936–2019).

Julie Flett

WE ALL PLAY

kimêtawânaw

GREYSTONE KIDS

GREYSTONE BOOKS • VANCOUVER/BERKELEY

Animals hide

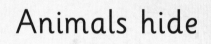

and hop

and sniff

and sneak

and peek

and peep.

We play too!
kimêtawânaw mîna

Animals swim

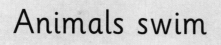

and squirt
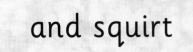

and bubble

and bend

and chase

and chirp.

We play too!
kimêtawânaw mîna

Animals slip

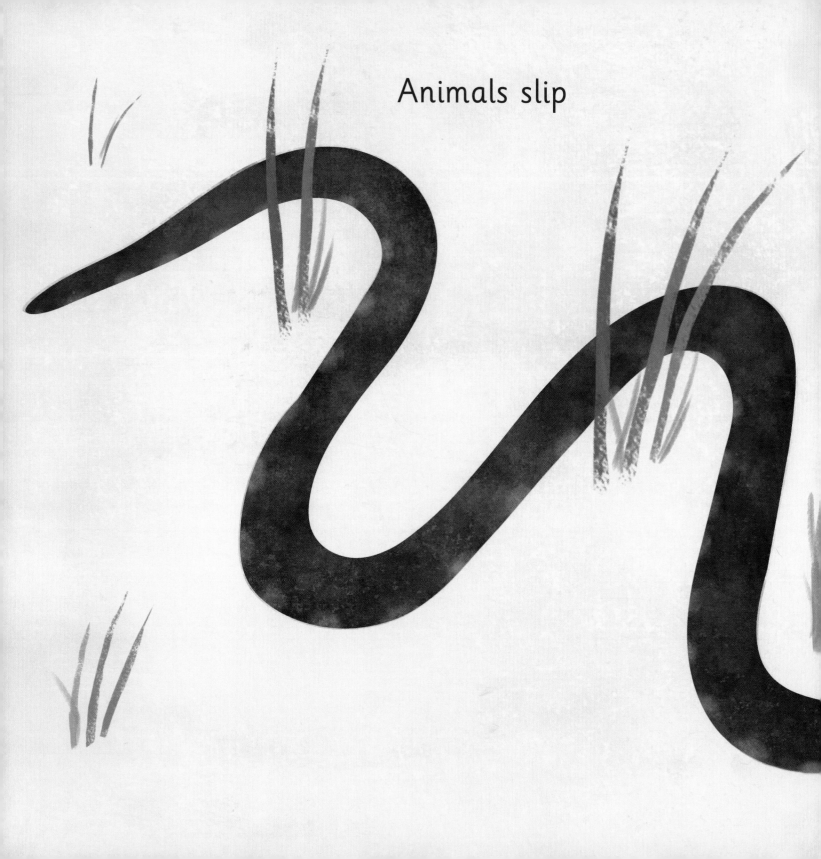

and slide

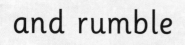

and rumble

and roll

and wiggle

and wobble.

We play too!
kimêtawânaw mîna

Animals rustle

and roost

and nudge

and nuzzle

and yip

and yawn.

And slowly, side by side,

animals fall asleep.

We do too.
nîstanân mîna
Zzzz . . .

LIST OF ANIMALS

ENGLISH	ONE	MORE THAN ONE	YOUNGER, SMALLER, CUTER
rabbit	wâpos	wâposwak	wâposos
fox	mahkêsiw	mahkêsiwak	mahkêsîs
turtle	mihkinâhk	mihkinâhkwak	mihkinâhkos
owl	ôhow	ôhowak	ôhos
beluga	wâpamêk	wâpamêkwak	wâpamêkos
seal	âhkik	âhkikwak	âhkikos
goose	niska	niskak	niskisis
bear	maskwa	maskwak	maskosis
bat	apahkwâcîs	apahkwâcîsak	—
wolf	mahihkan	mahihkanak	mahihkanis
bobcat	pisiw	pisiwak	pisîs
snake	kinêpik	kinêpikwak	kinêpikos
buffalo	paskwâwi-mostos	paskwâwi-mostoswak	paskwâwi-moscosos
child	awâsis	awâsisak	—
baby	oskawâsis	oskawâsisak	—

There are seventeen unique sounds in the Standard Roman Orthography (SRO) system used in this book. Short vowels sound much like the *a* in above, the *i* in bin and the *o* in book. Long vowels sound much like the *â* as in water, *ê* as in bay, *î* as in beep, and *ô* as in boat. The ten consonants—*p, t, c, k, s, m, n, w, y,* and *h*— sound much like their English counterparts, except for *c* which may sound like the "ch" in chat or the "ts" in cats, depending on local preferences. For example:

- kimêtawânaw—"we (all) play"—kih-may-TUH-waa-now
- kimêtawânaw mîna—"we (all) play too"—kih-may-TUH-waa-now MEE-nuh
- nîstanân mîna—"we do too"—NEESS-tuh-naan MEE-nuh

Audio pronunciations of the Cree words in this book are available on the book page for *We All Play* at greystonebooks.com.

Translation into Plains Cree (y-dialect) edited in Standard Roman Orthography by the Cree Literacy Network (creeliteracy.org).

DEAR READER,

Animals play. And we play too: kimêtawânaw mîna.

We all love to play. You may have played while you were reading this book. Maybe you played by sounding the words out in this book, saying them or signing them quickly and rhythmically, or getting up to jump and hop like the animals and kids in the story.

When I was growing up, my dad shared a lot about our relationship to animals and to each other, including the land, plants, beetles, the earth, wind, water, and sky. Whether we are running and hopping through the grass or rolling along the street or pondering creatures in the creek, we are all connected, living in relationship and in care to one another, in kinship. In Cree, this is called wâhkôhtowin.

I'm glad to be able to share some of this here with you hoppers and wigglers and wobblers and wanderers— and wonderers.

—Julie

Greystone Kids / Greystone Books Ltd.
greystonebooks.com

Cataloguing data available from Library and Archives Canada
ISBN 978-1-77164-607-9 (cloth)
ISBN 978-1-77164-608-6 (epub)

Translation into Plains Cree (y-dialect) edited in Standard Roman Orthography
by the Cree Literacy Network (creeliteracy.org)

Editing by Kallie George
Copyediting by Rhonda Kronyk, Hunter Cardinal, and Naheyawin
Proofreading by James Penco
Jacket and interior design by Sara Gillingham Studio

Printed and bound in China by 1010 Printing International Ltd.
The illustrations in this book were rendered in pastel and pencil, composited digitally.

Greystone Books gratefully acknowledges the Musqueam, Squamish, and Tsleil-Waututh peoples
on whose land our office is located.

Greystone Books thanks the Canada Council for the Arts, the British Columbia Arts Council,
the Province of British Columbia through the Book Publishing Tax Credit,
and the Government of Canada for supporting our publishing activities.